THE AMISH COWBOY'S CHRISTMAS

Large Print prequel novella

Amish Cowboys of Montana

ADINA SENFT

Cover design by Moonshell Books, Inc. via Canva.com and BookBrush.com. Images used under license.

German quotations from the 1912 Luther Bible, with English from the King James Version. "I Need Thee Every Hour," lyrics by Annie Sherwood Hawks, 1872, and "Peace, Perfect Peace," lyrics by Edward H. Bickersteth, Jr., 1875, now in the public domain. *Er hat ein Weib genommen,* translated by Adina Senft.

The Amish Cowboy's Christmas / Adina Senft—2nd ed. large print

ISBN 978-1-963929-20-1 R120324

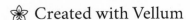 Created with Vellum

Praise for Adina Senft

"As with all this series, *The Amish Cowboy's Mistake* was fantastic. Adina Senft has a way of composing a storyline that not only holds your attention, but leaves you with a better outlook on your own faith, family, and overall perspective."

"Any book that can both entertain and leave me thinking is a book worth reading! Adina Senft is quickly becoming one of my favorite writers of Amish fiction.... Senft's characters are beautifully developed, [and] will move you to both laugh and cry."

In this series

AMISH COWBOYS OF MONTANA

THE AMISH COWBOY'S CHRISTMAS

Chapter 1
MOUNTAIN HOME, MONTANA

December, thirty years ago

TWO WEEKS before his sister's wedding, while jamming his black winter hat on his head, Reuben Miller opened the mudroom door off the kitchen at five in the morning and walked nose first into a wall of snow.

His hat fell off behind him. With a startled cry, he stepped on it as he backed away, and *Mamm* turned from the stove.

"Mercy! Close the door! Or it will all—"

Too late. The snow slumped inward as Reuben swung the door shut with all his strength. The heavy door crunched to a stop with a foot to go, the snow elbowing its way in like an unwelcome guest. Cold breathed through the gap, sending the temperature down in the kitchen behind him, though the woodstove's flue was wide open and it was nearly up to full temperature.

In all his twenty-two years on the rambling Montana property that his father was slowly turning into a working ranch, he had never seen snow like this. He'd heard tales of it—Annie Gingerich loved to tell the story of the ten-foot snow and how they'd had to climb out the second-story windows to milk the cows. But he'd never seen it with his own eyes.

Dat came into the kitchen and took in the scene at a glance. "Go get your brothers and sisters. This is going to take all of us."

Ten minutes later, his sister Lydia got busy with the broom and dustpan inside while Reuben, his father, and his brothers, Marlon and David, put on their snowshoes and attacked the intruding snow from the rear. By the time *Mamm* and his oldest sister Julia had finished cooking breakfast, a narrow path had been dug between shoulder-high banks of snow from the kitchen door out to the barn. They all squeezed back in, snowy and laughing, to eat.

"I'm surprised Little Joe Wengerd didn't tell us the weather was going to turn," Marlon said after their silent grace. He tucked into his bacon, eggs, and corned-beef hash with an appetite greater than usual. "He went into Mountain Home yesterday and would have heard the forecast at the hardware store."

"Unless it was a surprise to the weatherman, too," Lydia said. "Or Little Joe was distracted by Sadie, the eldest girl in that new family in the district. *Ach*, well. No harm done, except to Reuben's poor hat."

Reuben wasn't worried. Not about that, at least. "I'll just punch it back into shape. *Dat*, I wonder if we ought to check on the Glicks."

Julia, the sister closest to him in age, agreed instantly, since they had been friends all their lives, and all the Amish in the Siksika Valley looked out for one another. "Their house is nearly finished, but you know how the weather whistles through that little canyon behind them at the best of times."

His mouth full, *Dat* nodded. "Your own home first," he said around his hash. "We still have to make sure the near paddock is clear so we can get hay out to the cattle. And John Glick has that young relative of his working there. He's not short of help."

It would be a full morning's work on their own place, Reuben reflected, with no time left over to see if Naomi Glick was all right. Her father had built the family home in what he thought was a sheltering steep-sided valley, only to find out that it was more like a funnel for bad weather. Since no one had bought property out that way, nobody knew about its peculiarities.

It took until nearly noon to get the ranch set mostly to rights. It helped that, with the cloudy weather, the temperature had risen and a little of the snow had melted. With any luck, there wouldn't be any more surprise snowfalls overnight, and his mother and sisters could make their way from house to barn to sheds without wondering if they were going to be buried at any moment. When Reuben heard the county snowplow's engine grumbling along the highway, he could bear it no longer.

"Tell *Dat* I'm going over to the Glick place," he said to David.

"But it'll be dark in a couple of hours," his brother objected.

"I'll be home before then. Besides, I'm not taking a buggy. I'll go across country on the skis."

"Any particular reason you're so all-fired concerned about the Glicks?"

Reuben did not answer, only tugged on the ski shoes.

"I can think of a good reason." Julia's teasing voice floated over the row of horse stalls from the chickens' winter aviary on the other side.

"Never you mind," he called, stepping into the bindings. Then he tied the laces of his work boots together and hung them around his neck.

"And her initials are N.G." Fifteen-year-old Lydia, who was helping Julia clean the aviary, giggled as though she'd finally got one over on him.

He wouldn't give her the satisfaction of a protest or a denial. Instead, he glided out of the barn toward the long lane, which no one had shoveled and probably wouldn't for a couple of days. Reggie, their border collie, who was the best cattle dog Reuben knew, tried to follow.

"Not this time, Reg," he said. "It's too deep for you. Stay."

His legs and arms found their rhythm, his ski poles punctuating the snow at regular intervals beside the ribbon-thin tracks of his skis. The Glick place was about a mile down the county road in the direction of the little town of Mountain Home, on the side opposite the Miller ranch.

Naomi's father was a blacksmith, having chosen that trade as a young man. Not everyone could make a go of running cattle. Reuben's own father was a careful manager of money, but at the same time, had a good eye for an opportunity and an affinity for the high country. In the cattle business, it took all three to be a success. *Mamm* did the books, and Reuben must have inherited her head for numbers, because when she got busy with home and garden in the summer, she left the accounting to him.

He was glad for the experience. If it were up to him, he'd go in with *Dat* in full partnership. But Marlon was the eldest, so it was his choice to make first. As the middle brother, he might be doing the books for Marlon someday. But that was okay, too. Reuben couldn't think of anywhere he'd rather be than right here, on their growing ranch in this beautiful country that seemed closer, somehow, to *Himmel* and therefore to *der Herr*.

He glided to a stop at the Glick mailbox, or where he thought it should be now that the plow had thrown an additional few feet of snow over it. He dug down until he located it and slipped the mail out sideways. That Roy Beiler, who was about Marlon's age and was second cousin to John Glick, should have seen to this. Reuben tucked the mail into the pockets of his black wool coat and pushed on. The track down to the house was obliterated, but as he skied past the big shed that held the blacksmith shop, he could hear the regular ringing of a hammer on metal.

Someone had shoveled a path from house to shop, and another from shop to barn, but everywhere else was still pristine, though it was clear the family dogs had been bounding in the shallower drifts. If Naomi's father was working, surely Roy should be making the place passable for everyone else? Reuben came to a stop at the bottom of the steps leading up to the two-story house. It was a featureless gray rectangle except for its triple-paned windows and the wide-roofed porch that formed a deck in the front. Someday, the porch would have a railing and pickets, painted white as the *Ordnung* dictated, but for now the Glicks were lucky to have got the sidewalk poured before the first snow had fallen back in September.

He stuck the point of his pole into the ski bindings and popped them open, stood them in a drift beside the steps, and bounded up as though his feet were as light as his heart.

Maysie Glick, Naomi's youngest sister, dragged him inside, where the heat of the kitchen had him shucking coat and hat as fast as possible. Then he pulled on his boots.

"Mail's in the pockets," he said, and she squealed and began to empty all of them.

"*Mamm*, a circle letter from Ohio, a check

for *Dat*, *The Budget*, oh, a letter from our cousins in Pennsylvania, and what's this?"

Sharon Glick rolled her eyes and took the pale blue envelope from her daughter. *"Guder owed, Reuben, wie geht's?* Please excuse the rudeness of this child. I don't know where she gets her manners. The dogs, maybe."

"Mammmm!"

"We're all well, *denki*," he said with a smile. "I came to see that you were all right. Snow was so deep this morning we couldn't open the back door. I walked right into a wall of it."

Twelve-year-old Maysie's eyes went wide. "How did you get out? Dig?"

He nodded. "Took us all morning. I figured you might need some help over here—better late than never."

The Glick household was all girls. Not that they weren't capable and unafraid of hard work, but Reuben could imagine that for some tasks, John Glick could use an extra hand. Like clearing out all that snow between the buildings.

"Are you saying that nobody around here knows how to use a shovel?"

At the sound of her voice, Reuben's mouth dried up, and his tongue lost its ability to move.

Naomi Glick came into the kitchen with a pile of folded dish towels, her chin tilted at a challenging angle. Her hair was a glossy shade of brown, so dark it looked nearly black, drawn back into the bucket-shaped Montana *kapp* with a curl and a twist on the way. Her lashes were just as dark, and long enough to make a man lose his wits when he gazed into those blue eyes. Her cheeks were flushed from laundry day—laundry waited for nothing, not even a snowstorm—and on her nose there were seven freckles. Which he only knew because he had counted them one time when she was watching a pond hockey game and she didn't know he was standing behind her. She wore a green dress and a black bib apron, and looked so beautiful she stole his breath.

"Well?" Naomi raised one eyebrow at him.

He willed his mouth to open and words to come out. *"Neh,"* he croaked. "I brought your mail."

"Oh, did you?" She stuffed the dish towels into a drawer and, like a child, paddled through the pile at her mother's elbow. "It's here!" She held up the blue envelope and gave him a mock glare. "As if you didn't know."

As if he and David and Lydia hadn't helped Julia address a couple hundred of them this week. Maybe that was why his tongue was stuck to the roof of his mouth—it still tasted like the glue from the stamps.

Naomi slit the envelope as carefully as though she planned to re-use it, then drew a breath. "Oh, how pretty! And look at their names in silver. I've been hoping Julia would send me one for my keepsake book—but my goodness, Reuben, she didn't have to stamp it. I've been over there a dozen times lately."

As his sister's best friend practically since their mothers had come home from the hospital in the same week, Naomi would be joining Lydia as *neuwesitzer* on Julia's wedding day. Lydia was beside herself with excitement at such an honor, but all Reuben could think of was that for once, he had an excuse to be near Naomi for a whole day, with no one thinking it the least bit strange.

"It makes it official, I guess, to have a stamp on it," he managed.

But Naomi only made a sound in her throat that could have been agreement or disdain. Why couldn't he think of something witty and smooth to say? Something that would tell her how much it meant to him that she'd be part of such a happy day for their family?

That was the way of it, he thought with a sigh. At nine o'clock tonight, he'd think of the perfect response.

The thump of boots on the porch announced the arrival of Roy, who came in, having already swept off his pants and boots with the broom that had been standing next to the door. "How do, Reuben? Some snowfall, *nix?*"

"Ja," Reuben said. "I came to lend a hand."

Roy shook his head. *"Denki* for taking the trouble, but that's my job."

"Nonsense," Sharon Glick said. "Here, you two. Have some hot coffee and this carrot cake. It'll give you strength to take on the deck and the lane. Naomi and Grace have to go into town."

12

"Today?" Reuben said in astonishment. They wouldn't clear the lane for a couple of hours, and by then it would be dark.

"Tomorrow," Naomi told him firmly. "We have to buy blue napkins and silver ribbon to tie up the pieces of wedding cake."

Reuben and Roy looked at one another blankly. This made absolutely no sense.

Naomi and Sharon rolled their eyes at the hopelessness of men. "Your mother and Julia made extra fruitcakes to be cut up and given out as favors," Sharon explained. "The closer to the wedding date we come, the busier they'll be, so we volunteered to do it."

"There are four of us girls," Naomi said unnecessarily. "It won't take us long."

"I can help, too, if you need me." The words came out before his brain realized what his mouth was up to.

Roy gave a great bark of laughter. "That's women's work, Reuben Miller. Maybe I'd better get you out there in the snow. You need something more to do."

Reuben could feel his cheeks reddening, but he went without saying any more. He never minded helping out in the kitchen—they all did at home. No, he'd sacrificed his dignity on the altar of being able to do something with Naomi; he wasn't fussy about what it was, as long as he could be near her.

And now she probably thought he was an idiot—or a *faulenzer* trying to get out of yard work.

He and Roy made short work of the deck and turned their attention to the lane, which was probably a hundred yards long. Reuben eyed the sky.

"We'll get about half of it done," he said. "I can come back tomorrow well before the girls need to leave."

They bent to the labor, the shovels scraping in two different rhythms as they tossed the dry but still heavy high-country snow into the ditches on either side.

"Looking for reasons to come by, are you?" Roy asked.

Reuben wasn't sure what to say. "This would be hard for them, I think. Despite what Naomi says."

"I think you're sweet on her."

His face went cold—or maybe it was just the wind whistling down this odd little valley. "Don't need to be sweet on a girl to want to help out."

"You don't think I can do my job?"

Was he looking for an argument? Nettled, Reuben blurted out what was on his mind. "If you could, you'd've had this lane shoveled out this morning."

Roy snorted. "A lot you know. I was oiling harness and digging tracks around the yard and restringing the wash line in the basement for Naomi when the cord broke this morning."

Oh. "Sorry."

"She really appreciated that, and I was glad to do it for her, even though I had a lot of other work."

Reuben chose the better part and was silent.

Ten yards on, Roy mused, "I'd better go with the girls to town tomorrow. You never know if the buggy might get stuck."

For two seconds, Reuben wished he'd had the foresight to offer back there in the kitchen. "The county blade's been out."

"Still. Could be icy."

Reuben sped up his rhythm with the shovel to get out of speaking range. Roy would do what he wanted. But what he *couldn't* do two weeks from now was sit in the *eck* with the wedding party, or at the family table closest to it, where Reuben would be.

In fact, an urgency was building in his chest to speak to his sister Julia the moment he got home. For in the evening, after many of her wedding guests would have gone home, the *youngie* would still be there, waiting to see who the bride would pair them with for supper.

He had better make sure and certain that Julia's choice for Naomi wasn't Roy, or Little Joe, or any of the other young men in the district. He'd better make sure it was him.

Chapter 2

NAOMI DID her best to keep a sisterly smile on her face as Reuben and Roy went out to shovel snow. But it wasn't easy, and *Mamm* was not fooled.

"Looks like you've attracted some attention," she said casually after Maysie had gone downstairs to take the clothes off the line. The basement was warm, and the new woodstove seemed to be working well now that *Dat* had got the stovepipe fitted properly. The clothes dried almost before you finished hanging them all up. When they had been hung on the old line in the yard, they'd frozen hard as planks, and then you still had to dry them in the house once you wrestled them inside.

Her mind was rattling like an old buggy just so she wouldn't have to answer her mother. "Mm," she said. "Can I have another piece of cake?"

"Do you want to fit into that dress you just finished for Julia's wedding?"

With a sigh, Naomi covered the cake and put it back in the new propane fridge.

"Your father and I think Roy had better keep his mind on his work and not you," *Mamm* went on. She was as persistent as a deer trying to reach an apple, and there was no chasing her out of this particular orchard.

"He's only being nice," Naomi said, trying to sound noncommittal. As though it didn't matter. Better to talk about Roy than—

"And neither of those two are baptized." *Mamm* cocked an eyebrow at her. "Little Joe is, and so are the Yutzy twins. A man who is going in the right direction—"

"—is the man you want to walk beside," Naomi finished. "*Ja*, I know, *Mamm*. But I'm not interested in those boys."

"Why not?"

She tried to think why not. "I've known them all my life, mostly. They're like brothers to me. Friends to do things with, like play volleyball, and go fly-fishing and sledding."

"Many a friend has turned into something more, though, *liewi.*"

"So, you think that if it's meant to happen, it will happen?"

A moment too late, she realized that she hadn't avoided her mother's questions at all. She'd just answered her own.

Because it had happened. Reuben had happened, and Naomi didn't know what to do about it. Him. Anything.

"Has it?" *Mamm* asked casually.

"I don't know."

Which wasn't an answer, and *Mamm* knew it. But she didn't press the matter.

Instead, Naomi did the opposite of what she wanted to do, which was grab a shovel, tell Roy that her father wanted him, and help Reuben shovel the lane. She went downstairs to help Maysie take in the laundry and fold it and hang their dresses up and starch their *kapps*. Tasks she had done so many times that she didn't need to think about them.

She was free to think about Reuben, while Maysie chattered about the things that interested twelve-year-olds and not twenty-year-olds.

Reuben was twenty-one and hadn't yet joined church. Neither had she, but she planned to. What was keeping him? It couldn't be a desire for the world. He hadn't really done much of a *Rumspringe*—too much work on the ranch. You couldn't just walk away from cattle; no matter what season it was, they always needed something. Feed in winter, shots and brands in spring, rounding up and bringing down from the mountain allotments in autumn. But Reuben seemed content not to be kicking up his heels in town like some of the other boys.

She shook her head, wondering how the Amish boys on *Rumspringe* managed to find the *druwwel* they did. One or two had been in trouble with the sheriff for getting into a fight at the single bar their little town boasted. Another had tried to learn to drive a car and wound up in the Kootenai River. He was lucky he hadn't wound up in the hospital ... or the cemetery. Even Roy was in the habit of hanging around with the three young men of an *Englisch* family who had just bought five hundred acres up the road. They were wealthy and planned to turn an old farmhouse into a three-thousand-square-foot post-and-beam showpiece and raise prizewinning horses or some such thing.

So, it couldn't be a hankering for the pleasures of the world that was keeping Reuben from committing his life to God and the church. What was it?

She herself had decided she would talk to the bishop about beginning baptism classes in the New Year. She couldn't imagine herself not joining church. For goodness' sake, what had she been waiting for? A sign from Reuben that he was planning to do the same? A woman didn't make a choice as serious as that by waiting for someone else to do it; she had to make her choice for herself.

And that went for her choice of husband, too. Roy was a second cousin, a hardworking carpenter, easy to be with, and funny. If she hadn't already had Reuben on her mind, she might already have asked Julia to pair them up at the wedding supper. Maybe she should anyhow. That would throw *Mamm* off the scent for sure, and no one would think anything of it. He would be leaving once the house was finished in February, when they were to have church here. And Reuben would get the message that there might be other people interested in her, and maybe he ought to get off the fence and do something about it.

She sighed. No, that would be using poor Roy, and no girl with the Spirit in her heart would do that to a brother.

At the same time, there had to be a way to get Reuben's attention. The problem was, he was so shy he could hardly speak a word to anyone, let alone a girl. She'd tried to draw him into conversation before, and he'd been so uncomfortable he'd barely managed a *ja* or a *neh*.

Maybe he didn't even like her. Maybe he thought she wasn't womanly enough. She couldn't help it that she liked outdoor sports and yard work. She could knit, and sew well enough to make her own clothes, but a quilt with all its piecing and intricate stitching was just too much for her. Sometimes sitting still was too much for her.

She carried the folded clothes upstairs and took dresses, pants, and shirts into the various bedrooms. Some of the rooms weren't quite finished yet, but after their parents' was done downstairs Roy had finished hers and Grace's. All that was left now were Amy Jane's and Maysie's. She could still smell the paint on the windowsills and wainscoting when she walked in. *Dat* had made wrought-iron hooks for the back of the door and knobs for her white dresser, and *Mamm* had made thick window quilts for both windows. These rolled up during the day to let in the wide Montana sky, yet blocked out the cold night breathing against the glass. Her room faced east, so the sun woke her in summer and encouraged her in winter.

An idea whisked into her head with the speed of a mouse surprised by a chicken. Never mind Roy—what if she asked Julia to pair her up with Reuben at supper? Julia was her best friend. She'd never think that Naomi was being forward or too flirtatious asking for one particular boy. She'd be pleased.

At least, Naomi hoped she would be.

In any case, her secret would be out. But when it came to love, sometimes you had to drive outside the buggy tracks.

THE NEXT DAY, thank goodness, *Dat* had too many tasks on his list for Roy to go to town with Naomi and Grace, and they had the buggy to themselves. The snowplow had come by a second time, so the highway was clear and even dry in some spots. They stopped first at the Amish variety store, where Julia had placed her order for pale blue napkins and spools of narrow silver ribbon, and collected the lot, along with several rolls of cling wrap. Naomi also bought some pretty wrapping paper for the afghan she had knitted for Julia and Zeph Yoder as a wedding gift.

Knitting, at least, she could do well enough to make a gift.

When they rolled back down their lane, they found themselves following a second pair of buggy ruts into the yard, where a horse was visible through the open barn door, still hitched up but munching on a flake of hay.

"Company," Grace said happily. "I wonder who it is?"

Naomi had already recognized the Miller horse, but all she said was, "Let's find out."

They unhitched and put their own horse up in record time, and when they let themselves into the kitchen, Reuben Miller looked up from where he leaned on the counter, talking with *Mamm* and Maysie and sipping a cup of coffee. Naomi tried not to look as flustered as she felt while she emptied her shopping tote of its treasures.

"You brought over the cakes." She breathed in the rich scent of vanilla and fruit and marzipan from the cardboard boxes on the table. "I thought Julia was coming."

"I offered," Reuben said. "The letters are starting to arrive from the folks in other states, so she's got her big list out. When that comes out, you know you have to clear the decks."

"That's Julia." Naomi nodded. "I keep telling

her she needs one big book with all the lists in it, but—"

"—she says she can't carry it around." Reuben finished the sentence.

Naomi smiled at him just as he took a sip of coffee. Somehow, it went down the wrong way, and *Mamm* had to clap him on the back.

"Round up your sisters, Grace, while Naomi unwraps everything," *Mamm* said as though nothing had happened and Reuben's face wasn't red as a tomato. "Reuben, why don't you stay and help? That way, you can take all the wrapped favors home with you, and Julia can cross the job off that big list."

What was *Mamm* up to? Naomi wondered. Only yesterday she'd been cautioning her against getting interested in a man who wasn't baptized. And today she was inviting him to stay?

But somehow, *Mamm* managed not to see the questions on Naomi's face as she bustled around getting out knives and scissors. She even found a big plastic tub with a lid to store the wrapped pieces of cake.

"My goodness, where do we start?" Naomi

murmured as she gazed at the loaded kitchen table.

"With the cake," Reuben said. "You and I cut. Amy Jane wraps in cling wrap. Maysie wraps each piece in a napkin, and Grace cuts and ties the ribbon."

"A production line." Naomi's orderly brain was immediately impressed. "Let's get this going, then. *Mamm*, Grace is going to need some of your counter space."

Reuben sharpened the big kitchen knife and got to work pressing even cuts in a grid across the first cake. "Julia figured each cake would yield about a hundred pieces. What do you think?"

"Twelve by twelve? I think it's a good thing that knife is sharp and the cakes are still cold," Naomi said. "Maybe we should put the other two out on the porch."

"Good idea."

When she came back, she soon realized that Reuben didn't need her help, but fifteen-year-old Amy Jane did. The cling wrap had become far too affectionate with the poor *maedel* and was clinging to her hands and arms. The two of them soon worked out a system, though, and after that it was difficult not to turn the whole enterprise into a race.

"Slow down!" Grace laughed as they finished the second cake. "I can't get the ribbon tied fast enough for you."

"We need another person," Naomi agreed. "*Mamm?*"

"You might not mind dinner being late," *Mamm* said from the propane stovetop, "but your father might."

"What about Roy?" Maysie said. "He said he was going to put the hooks up in my room, but he hasn't yet. At least if he helps, he'll be inside. That's halfway to my room."

As though they had conjured him up, there was a thumping of boots, and Roy came in carrying one of the cake boxes. "Is there a reason this is sitting out in the snow?"

"To keep it cold, obviously," Amy Jane informed him. "Reuben, are you ready for the third one?"

"*Ja.*"

Reuben took the box from him while Roy took in the scene. "Guess you weren't joking yesterday, Reuben. Maybe I should try some kitchen work, too. After repairing the spring wagon, I could stand to be warm and dry for a bit."

And just like that, the sense of fun and camaraderie dissolved.

Which was strange, because usually Roy had them laughing over nothing at all.

Naomi tore off a piece of cling wrap with a sharp sound. "That's a *gut* idea. We were just saying we could use another pair of hands. If you take over here, I can cut Grace's ribbon for her, and we won't have a pile-up at the end."

Roy laughed and indicated the leather tool belt around his narrow hips. "Cling wrap or wainscoting and hooks in Maysie's bedroom? Can't do both at once. Maybe Maysie had better choose."

"Hooks," the little traitor said, hardly giving him a chance to finish his sentence.

"Hooks it is." He knocked on the top of her *duchly* as he passed, as though testing a melon, and she batted his hand away from her head as though she'd grown up with brothers.

"I won't be long here," Reuben said as Roy disappeared up the stairs. "I can cut ribbon."

It didn't take but a couple of minutes for the last pieces of cake to tilt under his knife, and he traded it for scissors. Grace told him how long the ribbon should be so she could curl both ends once the bow was tied, and they were back in production. But it didn't feel the same to Naomi. Because Roy could hear them from where he was working upstairs? But why shouldn't he do his work? Maysie had been waiting patiently to have the finishing done in her room, and he'd been working in the house every afternoon for a couple of weeks now.

And it wasn't as though he was mean or bad-tempered. Boys always teased each other. It was all in good fun.

But Reuben had gone back to his usual silence. Somehow, now that she'd seen him relaxed and part of this project that would add to his sister's big day, Naomi missed it. Roy's good-natured teasing had spoiled the fun when it should have added to the hilarity.

In another half hour, the last of the pieces of

cake made their way to the end of the production line, and the pretty bundles were carefully laid in the plastic bin for their trip to the Miller place.

"I'll come help you with the horse." Naomi pulled her wool coat off the coat tree, then opened the back door for him as he hefted the bin in both hands.

"I can do it."

"Then I'll help you with the cake."

"I can—"

"Back in a minute, *Mamm*," she sang, and followed him out anyway.

The sun was down behind the pines now, shining through the branches and laying slats of light on the snow.

"You'll get home before dark," she said, "but better light the lamps yet."

"Thanks for the help." He lifted the bin into the back of the buggy and tucked the buggy blanket around it so it wouldn't shift.

"Oh, ha-ha. Reuben, what's wrong?" Don't say *nothing*, she thought. Talk to me.

"Nothing."

With a sigh, she tried again. "Roy was just teasing. He does that to all of us. He has eleven brothers and sisters, and he grew up that way. Teasing. Joking. Making fun."

"I know."

But he wouldn't look at her. Instead, with sure hands on the horse's harness, he backed his patient animal out into the yard and turned her around.

Naomi marched around to the driver's side as he climbed in. "Aren't you going to let me thank you for helping us? It would have taken twice as long without you."

"You're welcome." He swallowed, gazing at something between the horse's ears. "I was glad to help. It was fun."

"It was," she agreed. "I've known you all my life, but I don't think I've seen you quite like that. Content. Laughing, even. It was *gut* to see you that way."

"Content to do kitchen work. *Ja*, that's me."

And suddenly she saw where the real trouble lay. Roy had not teased him. Roy had *shamed* him.

"That is an old-fashioned notion, Reuben Miller," she said, jamming her fists on her hips. "Work is work, no matter whether it's inside or outside. We needed your help, and you gave it without a moment's thought. That's what counts. I'd rather have a man who sees a job to be done and does it, than one who thinks the job is beneath him."

"Would you?" His hazel eyes met hers, and she suddenly heard her words ringing in the cold air as he must have heard them.

She blushed scarlet and stepped back.

"Naomi?" Roy called from the kitchen door. "Does Reuben need a hand with his horse?"

"*Neh*," she called over her shoulder. "If he did, I'd have lent him one."

Roy chuckled as he came down the steps, the tools in his belt clinking as he took it off. "You'd make a fine pair, Reuben in the kitchen and you in the barn. Drive carefully, now."

Reuben didn't reply. Instead, he clucked his tongue to his horse, and the buggy lurched into motion.

Roy was saying some nonsense to her, but

Naomi ignored him. She was too busy stomping up the steps and wishing her cousin would find some work that would take him away.

To the barn, maybe. Or better yet, farther away. Like Colorado.

Chapter 3

JULIA HADN'T EXPECTED to get the wedding favors back on the same day she had sent the cakes over. "This is *wunderbaar*!" she exclaimed, inspecting the neat stacks. "How pretty they are." She straightened in alarm with a sudden thought. "I forgot to buy a basket! To carry them from table to table."

"You have one," *Mamm* reminded her. "Wicker, *ja*? The one Annie Gingerich made for you is in the storage room under the stairs. I will be so happy to have my storage room back after Christmas."

At the moment, it was filled to its slanted ceiling with things for the wedding. Most of the basics came in the bench wagon—benches, silverware, plates—but Julia had been stockpiling tablecloths, centerpieces, salt and pepper shakers and a host of other things since she'd become engaged.

"I'll put this down in the pantry," Reuben said, hefting the bin once more. "I'm told it needs to be cool."

Julia followed him downstairs to make room in the pantry. While *Mamm*'s neat rows of canned sausage, tomatoes, pickles, and fruit filled one side, the other side had been designated for wedding supplies, including the fruitcakes that awaited the flowers that would be their final decorations for the *eck*. Reuben knew that several other households had set aside room in their pantries to help with the food for the wedding, too, and one entire freezer had been rented for the elk meat that the Montana Amish were using for both weddings this year instead of chicken roast. In their neck of the woods, sometimes you had to use what God sent you instead of what tradition dictated.

Clearly the *gut Gott* had sent Reuben this moment alone with his sister.

He set the tub of favors carefully on a shelf and made certain the lid was tight. Then he turned. "I have a favor to ask, *schweschder*."

"Name it," she said recklessly. "I can't believe you and the Glicks got this done so quickly. What a relief to have it off my mind."

"Will you put me with Naomi Glick for supper?"

Julia gazed at him, his busy, organized sister stricken to stillness for once. Reuben felt a pang of alarm. This was not the laughing agreement he'd expected. Or even the teasing. This was *Ach neh, I've made a mistake.*

"Has she already asked you for a supper partner?" he got out. He felt sick. Two weeks to go, and he was already too late.

"*Neh,*" Julia said slowly. "She hasn't. But … but Roy Beiler asked me last week, at church. And I said I would. I didn't know—"

Didn't know you cared. He heard the end of the sentence as clearly as if she'd said it.

"It's all right," he said. He couldn't stand to see that stricken look in her eyes. "I guess I should have asked you sooner." Like right after she got engaged. Who made sure of their partner nearly a month before a wedding?

Roy Beiler, evidently. No wonder he'd had that careless confidence around Naomi. He'd known all along that he had one up on Reuben.

"It isn't all right," Julia said. "I should have asked you ages ago if there was anyone you'd prefer. I feel terrible. You're *mei bruder*. I'd far rather you were with Naomi than Roy." She gazed up at him as though trying to convince him of something. "I know he's sweet on her. And … oh, Reuben, I'm sorry to say this, but … maybe this isn't such a mistake after all. I—I think she's sweet on him, too."

Reuben swayed and actually took a step back so that the shelving would act like a bracing arm. "What makes you say that?"

Julia shrugged helplessly. "Oh, I don't know. The way they always sit across the table from one another at singing. Like, right across. I saw her handing around a plate of whoopie pies this past Sunday, and she served him first. Little things that a woman notices about another woman, especially when she's your best friend."

He'd had no idea. Hadn't seen any of those things, and he could feel Naomi's presence in a room even when he wasn't looking. And then this afternoon—had he really misread her so badly? She'd said she'd rather have a man who helped without being asked, and then she'd looked right at him and blushed. He could swear it was a blush, not the normal rosy cheeks of someone outside in the cold in December.

But maybe he was just clueless. Maybe he should stick to cows and forget about women.

Julia touched his arm. "I put you with Grace Glick. I hope that's all right."

"It's fine. We get along well. Don't worry about it."

But he could feel her gaze between his shoulder blades as he left the cool side of the basement and closed the door so the heat from the warm side wouldn't get into the pantry. His throat was tight. His eyes burned.

He must be coming down with something.

SUNDAY EVENING, the Miller family gathered in the big living room where church would be held next week, and where the wedding would be held the Tuesday after that, so the bench wagon wouldn't have to move between homes if the roads were bad. From tomorrow on, every day was going to be busy, cleaning the house from top to bottom and repairing anything that needed it, to say nothing of making sure the barn was cleaned and shipshape and all the fences checked for loose wire. Reuben could imagine Julia's dismay if her wedding were interrupted by the cattle getting out on the county highway or some similar disaster. The community would bring it up for years, the way Annie told the story of the snowstorm.

But for this evening, there was only the cozy warmth of a weathertight house and the comfort of his family. Only Julia knew the reason he was even less talkative than usual.

They were reading their way through Isaiah and his prophecies about Jesus, in preparation for Christmas.

But he was wounded for our transgressions, he was bruised for our iniquities: the chastisement of our peace was upon him; and with his stripes we are healed.

Dat read from Chapter 53 in his sonorous voice that Reuben could easily imagine being that of the prophet. When he concluded, *Mamm* took up the next verse, then Marlon, Julia, Reuben, David, and Lydia, who concluded the chapter. Something about the words, so full of hope and beauty, calmed him. Made him realize there was more to life and his own service to God than his small hopes and dreams.

If it's Thy will that she spends her life with someone else, Lord, help me to be willing for it. Help me to be a good friend to her even if she doesn't choose me. I pray You would guide me in the way I should go and lead me to the one You have chosen to be my partner in life. In Jesus' name, Amen.

———

A KITCHEN SHOWER for Julia was held on Tuesday at the Wengerd ranch across the county highway from the Miller place, hosted by Little Joe's mother and sisters. The men were having a work party at the Miller place in a whirlwind of repairs and painting. Naomi and Lydia, as Julia's bridesmaids, were the hostesses, while their mothers and Zeph's looked on, and the women of the community came to make sure that Julia began her new life with everything she needed.

That didn't mean a few clever pranks weren't played, though, or that the girls didn't get away with more jokes and laughter than they would ever dare if the men were present. Naomi's sides ached from laughing even as she hustled in and out of the Wengerd kitchen with plates of goodies and pots of coffee and tea. Lydia acted as official recorder for the thank-you notes as Julia unwrapped each gift—a set of measuring cups and spoons, a set of mixing bowls, a breadboard handmade with strips of light and dark woods, and at least half a dozen tablecloths, one of which was like a thinly batted quilt so intricately pieced it made the circle of young women gasp as Julia unfolded it.

"I will never serve food on this," Julia vowed,

hugging Priscilla Yoder, her future sister-in-law, who had spent all autumn making it. "If someone spilled gravy or coffee on it, I'd burst into tears."

"I hope you find another way to use it, then," Priscilla said softly. "It's completely washable, so it will come to no harm."

When the gifts had been opened and the young women had settled in to chatter and catch up on local news now that the weather had improved and people could get around again, Naomi ran into Julia coming out of the bathroom.

"I need to talk to you," she said, dragging her best friend back in and closing the door.

While Naomi balanced on the edge of the clawfoot tub, Julia closed the toilet lid and sat on it. "What's going on? And by the way, thank you again for wrapping all the cake favors. I know it was a huge job, but Reuben says that at least you all had fun doing it."

"We did, and you're most welcome." Naomi tried to find a comfortable spot on the edge of the tub. "But I wanted to ask you something."

"After all you're doing for me? Anything."

"Can you put me with Reuben for the supper?"

Julia slowly closed her eyes as though she'd just gotten bad news instead of a question that she must have been asked a dozen times today alone.

"What? What is it?" Naomi's fingers curled over the edge of the tub.

"I have just made the world's biggest mistake." Julia gazed at her, her brown eyes pinched with regret.

"How?" Naomi asked. "Here? Today?"

"No," Julia groaned. "I thought you were sweet on Roy Beiler. So, when he asked me to put you two together, I told him I would."

Naomi leaped to her feet at this double disaster. "Sweet on *Roy*?"

Julia covered her face with both hands, then peeked between her fingers. "I thought you liked him. I've seen you together. Sitting across from each other at singing, you doing little things for him, him doing little things for you…"

Naomi's astonishment made her sit down

again, gripping the rim of the tub. "When has he ever done anything for me?"

"Why, you said that he built a bookshelf in your room. None of your sisters have one. I've seen it."

"I have more books than my sisters do, and they're tired of tripping over the piles when they try to open the windows. Amy Jane was the one who asked him to put shelves in for the sake of her own stubbed toes, not for my benefit."

"Well, what about all those times he drove you home from singing?"

"We live on the same place!"

Julia put up her hands. "So, you're saying that you don't really like him?"

Naomi tried to be fair, even though her plans had crashed into pieces. After all, Julia had thought she was doing something that would make her happy. "He's my cousin."

"Second cousin. Once removed. Or something."

"Still. I like him the way anybody likes their relatives." She waved her hands helplessly. "Or the way I like ... Joe Wengerd, or any of the other boys. They're my brothers in the church. Nothing more."

"Oh, dear." Julia heaved a sigh. "Well, there's no getting out of it now. If it's any comfort, Reuben wanted to be your supper partner, too."

Naomi nearly went over backward into the tub. "He did?"

Julia nodded. "I know I'm not supposed to tell in advance, but I told him I'd already put you with Roy. He's going to be with Grace."

"So, he knows I'm partnered with Roy," she said, just to make sure.

A pained look crossed Julia's face. "That's where I made my mistake, *liewi*. I told him I thought the two of you were sweet on each other."

Oh, no. Naomi's heart picked up its pace. "What did he say?"

"Nothing. Absolutely nothing. I don't know if that's good or bad."

"That's Reuben," Naomi said.

And now she was confused all over again. Did he not care that Roy had got ahead of him? Or was it perfectly fine that now the *Gmay* would have no chance to cast speculative looks at them and wonder if they'd become a couple? She sighed. With Reuben, it was impossible to know what he was thinking, and she just didn't have the courage to ask him outright.

"Thanks for telling me, anyway," she said to Julia, and rose.

"I'm sorry I got it all mixed up."

Naomi hugged her. "It's all right. There's still the Gingerich wedding in the New Year."

"What if Roy has spoken to Lorena Gingerich already?"

"He wouldn't," Naomi said. Would he? Oh, goodness. "It's different in Holmes County or Lancaster, where weddings go on from October to February and people go to three in one day. Who pays attention if a boy and girl happen to get paired up more than once? But here?" Julia knew as well as she did the talk that such a thing would cause. No. Roy wouldn't do that. "What kind of man would put me in that position?"

"One who wants to push you into a public show of some kind," Julia replied.

She had always been clever about figuring

people out. Naomi just wished she had not been quite so clever this time.

"All he has to do is ask, if it's a date he wants," Naomi pointed out. "Mind you, I'd say no."

"Maybe he thinks that this way, you'll have to say yes."

"He doesn't know me very well, then." Naomi could feel a frown forming between her brows. She tried to relax, but this was not a relaxing situation. "What am I going to do?"

"Well, I can't rescind a promise," Julia told her unhappily. "Do we know if Roy is sweet on anybody for sure? You could trade places. People do that all the time."

But neither of them could think of anyone he'd been courting. He didn't drive any special person home after singing—most of the time, he simply took the Glick girls home the way they had all come together. He didn't have his own buggy because he was only here until the house was finished, so it wasn't like he had the freedom to go courting, anyway.

"I guess I'll just have to be graceful about it," Naomi finally conceded. "At least it's only supper. We don't have to stay partners for the singing or for the *fress*."

"True," Julia said, nodding. "But I'll tell you what. When we get home tonight, I'll let Reuben know I was wrong."

Naomi wasn't sure it would matter to him one way or another, given his lack of reaction to the news in the first place. "Keeping things truthful would be *gut*," she said. "No matter what Reuben thinks, the last thing I want is for a rumor to get out that Roy and I are courting."

"Leave that part to me," Julia said as someone knocked on the door and demanded whether the bride-to-be was still in there. "And if you want a little hint, you might be a tiny bit forward with my brother. He's the nicest and best man in the world, but he is shy and quiet to a fault."

"I did notice that." Naomi opened the door and summoned up a smile. "Look who I found!" she said to the girls outside, half of whom probably thought this was another prank. "The future Zeph Yoder *sei* Julia!"

Be a tiny bit forward with my brother.

Later, as Naomi drove home with her

mother, Grace, and Amy Jane, she despaired of being able to do that. An outdoor girl she might be, and able to stand up for herself … but when it came to someone who mattered, she was discovering, she was as closed up and shy as Reuben himself. And besides, he might not like it if, all of a sudden, she was dropping over to the Miller place and finding reasons to talk to him, or sitting close enough at singing that she could catch his eye and smile every time he looked up. The very thought of behaving that way and losing his respect just made her curl up inside.

But what to do?

She couldn't go to her mother and ask for advice. *Mamm* wasn't that kind of woman. She was brisk and businesslike and would probably say, "For goodness' sake, *dochder*, leave all that up to *der Herr* and come help me clean the chicken coop."

Naomi was doing her best to leave it up to *der Herr*. But maybe He in His wisdom had already given her a hint. Reuben, after all, had asked his sister to partner him with Naomi. So, if the gate was open, maybe all she had to do was walk through it.

But how?

That evening, after they had listened to *Dat* read a story aloud from the *Martyr's Mirror* and everyone had said good night, Naomi sat on her bed with the Bible.

Lieber Vater, I need your guidance. Show me the way I should go that will put me safely in Your hand.

Randomly, she slid her thumb between the thin pages and opened it, closed her eyes, and plopped her finger somewhere on a page. Then she opened her eyes to see it was the first chapter of Paul's letter to the Romans.

Making request, if by any means now at length I might have a prosperous journey by the will of God to come unto you.

She gazed at the words a long time, then marked the page with a bit of Julia's silver ribbon and blew out the lamp. *A prosperous journey.* A month ago, she had been over at the Millers' for what Lydia called The Great Cake Baking Date, compounding the wedding cakes, which had to be done weeks in advance. Julia had mentioned that after their honeymoon visits here in Montana, she and Zeph might travel to Whinburg Township to visit relatives they both had there. "Zeph made enough money at the cattle auction that he can afford tickets and expenses for us both," she'd said. "You'd be welcome to come, Naomi, and Grace as well, if your parents can send you. My brother Marlon is thinking of it, too."

"Go with you on your honeymoon?" Naomi had asked in astonishment.

"It's fairly common in the larger settlements," Julia's mother had said with a smile. "Wouldn't you love to go to Pinecraft, for instance, with one of your best friends as chaperone? You'd be surprised how many of the *youngie* make up a small party with the newlyweds and travel together."

Naomi had laughed the idea away. Nobody here did that, mostly because travel to and from the young settlements in Montana wasn't easy, and many families couldn't afford the cost for the bride and groom, never mind half the wedding party.

She hadn't given it a thought from that moment to this. But what if she did go ... and Julia convinced Reuben to go, too?

Naomi relaxed back into her pillow and tried to imagine it. Traveling on the train together. Enjoying the red rocks of the Southwest, the infinite fields of the central states, the old settlements of Pennsylvania as they slid by the windows of the observation car. Eating breakfast in the dining car, and in between, talking as they never got the chance to on Sundays or during work frolics.

The more she thought about it, the more she became convinced that this was the direction in which the *gut Gott* was pointing her. It was crazy, and outlandish, and she had no idea whether *Mamm* and *Dat* would even have the money to send her. But at least she could try, couldn't she? You never got anywhere if you didn't try.

The moon rose and painted a silvery bar of light on the opposite wall. The wedding was a week from today, and Christmas a few days after that. The newlyweds would probably make their local wedding visits in the New Year, so if a trip were to happen, it might not be until nearly February.

Could she bide her time until then? Or had Julia advised her to be a little bit forward for another reason?

Naomi drew a deep breath and let it go. There was only one place to find answers when the whole world seemed to be a series of question marks. She slid off the bed and knelt beside it to pray.

Chapter 4

NO MATTER THE joys and disappointments that life threw at you, Reuben thought, you could always count on some things. Like the beauty of God's creation. The sunrise. And cows.

After all the scrubbing and painting was done, the last thing on his parents' extensive list was riding fence to make certain that every length of barbed wire and every post was fit to last the winter. Of course, they'd checked the miles of fence before they'd brought the cattle down from the grazing allotments in September. But *Dat* was still concerned the snow and the low temperatures this month might have done some damage.

So here they were, Reuben and his brothers and father, the Friday before church and before the wedding, riding fence just to make sure.

Reuben's section was closest to the county highway, where anything might have happened, from a deer miscalculating a jump over the fence to a drunk driver crashing into it, then backing out and driving away. And sure enough, here was a swath cut through the snow piled on the roadsides, as though someone had used the snowbank to slow down instead of their brakes. It hadn't worked—a couple of fence posts had been yanked out of the ground with the impact and left lying there, trailing wire for fifty feet on either side.

What were the odds that the culprits had been the boys from the *Englisch* horse outfit up the road with their big Ford F-150 truck? No rancher in cattle country would leave fencing on the ground if he were at fault. But neither would an Amish man go marching up to an *Englisch* truck to check for scratches on the bumper. No, he would simply repair the fence in silence and hope that one day the culprits would see the error of their ways before they hit more than just a fence post with their vehicle.

"Whoa, Tim," he said to his cutting horse. "There might be some grazing here that the cattle haven't got to yet. Reggie, *kumm mit*. Not out on the road. We'll stop here for a while."

He looped the reins around a post, brushed the snow away from the grazing, and took down two of the new posts tied to the back of his saddle. His tools were in the saddlebag. The old posts were done for, so he dug up their bases with the small spade and replaced them. It took a little time to re-string the barbed wire, to the point that he even worked up a bit of a sweat in the bright sun. It wasn't warm by any means, but the sun was sure welcome.

When Reggie barked, he looked up.

"Hallo, Reuben Miller." Roy Beiler pulled up the Glick spring wagon in the road. He couldn't pull off, since the shoulder was buried somewhere under the snowbanks.

"Roy," Reuben greeted him, twisting wire with expert fingers. "Looks like an *Englisch* vehicle came to a sudden stop here in our fence."

"*Ja*, that was the Taylor boys last night."

"Would've been nice if someone had let us know. It was only by chance we didn't turn the winter stock into this pasture."

"*Ja*, it would have," Roy agreed, as if the hint had flown right past him with the speed of a hummingbird.

Then again, it probably had.

"Wedding's coming up pretty quick, hey?" the young man went on.

"Got to get all the fences checked so that none of the cattle escape and spoil Julia and Zeph's day." *Like this spot right here*, he didn't add.

"I haven't been to a Montana wedding. I suppose it's much like weddings anywhere, with the bride pairing people up at supper?"

"I suppose."

"Do you think your sister has paired me up with anyone?"

Reuben wasn't touching that with a four-foot fence post. "You'd have to ask her."

"Oh, I already did." He waited for Reuben's

response, but Reuben kept his mouth firmly shut. "Want to know who I put in a request for?"

He didn't need the other pair of wire snips, but Reuben walked over to Tim and got them out of the saddlebag all the same, then bent to give Reggie a pat to dip out of view of the human gadfly on the road.

"At home, you can pretty much count on lots of romances getting their start at the wedding supper every year," Roy mused aloud. "Is it the same here?"

"Don't know." Reuben snipped the wire close. Then he moved on to the wire above it. Their fences had three rows of wire, because *Dat* was a cautious man and did a job properly the first time. The fence would stand up to a cow, but not much could stand up to a joyriding pickup truck.

"Naomi mentioned something interesting this morning at breakfast," Roy said.

Reuben cocked an eye at him. "Ain't you got somewhere to be? Some of us have work to do."

"Aw, I just stopped to shoot the breeze. I hear there might be some going on the

honeymoon trip with Julia and Zeph, that's all.
I'll just be on my way."

Julia had been talking about it just that
morning at breakfast, and Marlon seemed to be
getting more serious about going along. Do not
ask if Naomi is thinking about it, too, he told
himself. Reuben clamped his mouth shut and
bent to wrap the wire around the post. Do
not ask.

Roy picked up the reins. "I have half a mind
to ask John Glick if I can have two weeks off,
and go along. I have a couple of uncles in
Whinburg Township I haven't seen since I was
as old as Maysie. It would be *gut* to see them
again … and then there's the train trip *allll* the
way across the country."

His tone made it sound like the trip would
take weeks. Weeks of traveling and seeing new
things with … whom?

Roy, clearly disappointed that his bombshell
was a dud, flapped his reins over the Glick
horse's back. "Well, better get these building
supplies where they're supposed to be. Nice
talking to you."

With a grunt, Reuben went back to his work.

But as soon as the spring wagon crested the hill and went into the dip on the other side, he put both gloved hands on the new post and hung his head between his arms. Reggie trotted over and gazed at him anxiously.

Long breaths made puffs of cloud in the cold. Roy was just saying these things to get Reuben's goat. John Glick would never allow him to take those weeks off with the house still unfinished and John and Sharon's turn to host church coming up. Even Reuben knew February was the unofficial deadline for the house's interior to be completed, painted, and spit shined in preparation for the Lord's presence and that of the *Gmay*.

"It's okay, boy," he said to the dog. There was still hope.

———

THE CLEAR WEATHER held for church on Sunday. The sun was still thinking about rising as the Glicks climbed into the big family buggy at eight o'clock, but later, by the time the young men and boys filed into the Miller house and found their places, it had cleared the mountains and shone in through the living room windows like a blessing.

Naomi hoped the skies would still be that fathomless blue for the wedding on Tuesday. Maybe she should ask Little Joe after church if he'd heard the weather forecast. Involuntarily, she turned her head to locate his tall form behind the married men, and instead, her gaze found Reuben's.

A shock rang through her body, as though she were a bell and someone had struck her softly with a mallet. Hastily, she bowed her head and hoped that no one had seen. She could still see his eyes, though, so steady and warm, as though the sight of her was all he needed just then. A Christmas present he had been looking forward to.

And oh, wasn't she just so *hochmut* this morning, thinking such a thing!

The sermon before Christmas was always Matthew 4 and 5, about the end of the world. The Amish year began with the Christmas sermon about the birth of Christ—the beginning of the New Testament and a new salvation. Naomi listened to the verses as Bishop Bontrager read them and tried to keep her mind on all the ways in which Scripture focused not on this world, but on the next.

The way she was supposed to.

It wasn't easy when she could feel Reuben's gaze on her even yet. She'd never had this feeling before, as though there were a piece of wire between them, and every time he moved, it tugged on her, too. If Julia hadn't told Naomi that Reuben had asked for her, how long would she have gone on, thinking he was such a good catch for a woman, but not having the courage to believe it could be her?

Maybe they wouldn't be partners for the wedding supper, but as the saying went, it was the thought that counted. Oh my, the thought had changed everything. *Be a tiny bit forward with my brother,* Julia's voice whispered in her memory. Naomi didn't quite know how to do that, but she would figure it out. That look over her shoulder had been a beginning. And he'd met her halfway, hadn't he? Even if he hadn't meant to.

After the last hymn, the bishop announced

that everyone was invited to the wedding on Tuesday and also to the Gingerich wedding in the New Year. And then it was time for the men to turn the benches and tables around for the fellowship meal and for Naomi to get busy helping the Miller women get the food on the tables. The families had organized casseroles today, including their own—a rich, cheesy one with homemade tomato sauce and venison and pork sausage. The *Gmay* in Mountain Home was not that large—only fifteen families—so they all fit comfortably in the sitting room and dining room.

After lunch, the women did the dishes. and the men put them away in the bench wagon along with the benches. Then the wagon was put into the barn, ready for Tuesday.

Tuesday! Even though Naomi didn't have to speak or do anything but sit beside Julia in support, it would still be exciting to sit at the front of the church, and then in the *eck* for the wedding meal after the service.

Had Julia kept her promise and told Reuben that Naomi had asked for him, too? To be sure, she would help Reuben see that he had been her first choice. But how? She found her coat and gloves at the bottom of the pile in the downstairs bedroom. She always thought better outside.

As she crossed the yard, some of the men were standing in a circle at the barn door, their breath coming in faint clouds as they talked over the events of the week and speculated on whether the weather would hold. Small boys ran here and there in gaggles—maybe there was a litter of kittens in the hayloft. She half expected Reggie to come lolloping up to go with her, but he was nowhere in sight. Probably little boys were more exciting for a dog than one lone girl heading off down the lane for some time to think.

The snow had melted in big patches, which meant there was enough grazing for the buggy horses to be turned outside in the paddock. She leaned on the rail fence that ran down both sides of the lane. Montana in winter had its own bleak splendor, but her favorite season was late spring, when the mud and slush gave way to grass and meadow flowers. When the birds returned from the south, and the air was alive with song. When the cows had safely calved and were ready to go with their mothers up to the high pastures and spend the summer getting fat before they were brought down and sent to market. When—

Something that wasn't a buggy horse or a cow caught her eye out in the pasture. She straightened. An animal? Was it hurt? And then she heard a distant whine, as though its strength were nearly gone.

Oh, goodness. It was Reggie!

Without another thought, she gathered her Sunday skirts, climbed the rail fence, and dropped lightly to the other side. The pasture was mushy from the melt, and water seeped into her black Oxfords and through her black stockings, but she hardly felt it. She tried to keep to higher ground and zigzagged her way over to the border collie, who was lying hunkered in a clump of grass, shivering.

"Reggie! *Ach*, you poor thing."

She saw immediately what had happened. A fight—probably with a coyote who was getting too close to the livestock. Reggie's shoulder was bloody, and there were puncture marks just above the joint in his right hind leg.

"It's okay, boy. You're too heavy for me to pick up, but I'm going to get help. Don't you worry."

She straightened—turned—and practically walked into Reuben Miller.

"Coyote?" he asked, holding her steady.

"I think so. He needs help." She felt the loss of his gentle touch when he pulled away and bent beside the dog.

"I saw him after breakfast, but not since. David usually puts him in the barn to keep him from barking at the horses. Poor guy, he's just trying to herd them. Come on, old friend," he said, scooping the forty-pound dog into his arms. Poor Reggie let out a yelp, but then licked Reuben's face as though he knew he hadn't hurt him on purpose. "You did well, protecting our cows from that coyote. I hope he came out worse than you did."

"Of all the animals on the range out here, coyotes are the ones I like the least," Naomi said, setting off beside him. "They're so sneaky and cowardly."

"And smart," Reuben added. "I've seen them gang up on an elk and come at it like the points of a triangle, all closing in. Luckily that cow elk had some pretty hard hoofs on her, and she got away. She was pregnant, too."

"Do you think we'll be able to help Reggie?" Naomi asked anxiously, rubbing the dog's ears. "We'll never get the vet out here on a Sunday."

"*Dat* wouldn't call the vet for a dog, even a good one like Reggie," Reuben said. "We'll do what we can for him. Get the gate, would you?"

They'd crossed the pasture on a diagonal that brought them to the barnyard gate. Once inside, Reuben led her into an empty stall, where she spread some hay, and he lowered the dog into it.

"If you get some water to wash him, I'll dig through our livestock medicine cabinet and see what we have," Reuben said.

"Bandages, do you think?"

"Maybe, for the leg. Not sure about that shoulder. Might have to stitch it up. But we'll wash it out first and see."

Naomi turned to go.

"Naomi—*denki*," he said, joining her at the door of the stall. "If not for you, he'd have lain out there all day. We wouldn't have missed him until suppertime, and the cold would have got him by then."

"I'm just glad I saw him. I hope we can help. He's such a good boy and does his job without complaint."

"Why were you out there?" he asked, a tiny, puzzled pleat between his brows.

If they had an hour, she'd tell him. But they didn't. Reggie needed them. "I'll tell you when we get Reggie fixed up."

The puzzlement melted into a smile. "All right. That's a promise."

There was a cement sink in the utility room next to the tack room, and while there was no way to heat the water without going into the house, at least there was a white porcelain basin and a pile of rags neatly folded on the shelf above the sink. As in any Amish home out here, nothing was thrown away until it had fulfilled every possible purpose. These rags had once been flannel sheets, shirts, and dishtowels. She chose a couple and returned to the stall, where she wet one and flushed the blood from Reggie's wounds.

"You've just been punctured, boy, not slashed," she murmured to him. "I think we can get away without stitches, because trust me, my sewing skills are bad enough on fabric, never mind on a good boy like you."

"Good thing he knows you like him," Reuben said, coming in with his hands full of tins and a bottle of iodine. "Your bedside manner could use some work."

She grinned at him and stuck out the tip of her tongue because she was a mature woman and not a little girl who would stick out the whole thing.

Reuben seemed to almost be smiling as he chose some salve, and she handed him a clean rag. Poor Reggie did his best to be brave, but a whimper or two got out all the same when the iodine went on, and she stroked his head. "Good boy," she crooned. "You're a good boy."

When he'd salved all the dog's wounds, Reuben glanced at her. "Bandages?"

She shook her head. "When the vet came to

treat one of the buggy horses, he didn't bandage him up. He said the air would help it heal faster."

Reuben nodded. "Horses aren't so likely as dogs to lick and worry at their wounds, though."

Naomi considered this. "Maybe just the leg."

Reuben bandaged the leg with a length of old pillowcase and knotted it with what looked to Naomi to be a great deal of skill. "Guess he'll be in here for a day or two, until he's not so sore."

"It's plenty warm," Naomi agreed. "And we'll get his water and food dish."

They put away the salves and rags and closed the stall door, then folded their arms along the top as they gazed at Reggie. With a sigh of relief that it was all over, the dog put his head on his paws and closed his eyes.

"About that promise," Reuben said.

Naomi swallowed. "I went down the lane a bit to think. I think better outside. I was standing just like this at the fence, and I saw him out there in the pasture."

"And what would take a bridesmaid away

from my sister and all those *maedscher* inside, talking a mile a minute about the wedding?"

She huffed a laugh. "Do you know, I clean forgot about the wedding. What a terrible *neuwesitzer* I'm turning out to be. Getting the wrong partner at supper was just the beginning."

Silence fell, punctuated by the lowing of the cows outside, the clop and swish of horses, and the chickens hunting in the hay in their aviary.

When Naomi could stand it no longer, she looked up at him. He was gazing down at Reggie, chewing on his lower lip.

Be a tiny bit forward with my brother.

Have your loins girt about with truth, Paul had told the Ephesians.

"I asked Julia if she would partner me with you," she said. When he didn't move, she added, "But Roy had got there first, and she couldn't break her promise."

His hands had been clasped loosely as they hung over the door, but now they flexed and gripped each other as though Reuben were in the throes of a struggle. "He beat me to it, too,"

72

he croaked. "When I asked my sister to pair us up."

Us. What a beautiful word. In an upwelling of unexpected happiness, Naomi didn't know whether to sing or cry.

"The best laid plans, huh?" she said hoarsely. "And now he tells me he's thinking of going along on the honeymoon trip. It's enough to make a person want to stay home."

At last, one side of his mouth quirked up. "It's enough to make *me* want to go to Alaska."

She laughed and the tension broke. "I hope you don't. I hope you stay right here. Reggie needs you."

"Just Reggie?" he asked, so quietly she hardly heard him, even though he was standing right next to her.

"And the cows," came out of her mouth, like an idiot.

"Naomi." Oh, his voice, as though he were on the last thread of his endurance. Her heart melted.

"And me," she whispered. "Me, most of all."

And then somehow, he turned and she

turned and his arms went around her and there were two thick winter coats in this hug, but it didn't matter. By some miracle, she was exactly where she wanted to be, and nothing in this world had ever felt so right.

Chapter 5

A WEDDING, Reuben was amazed to discover, was a completely different occasion when you were in love. And it was even more miraculous when that love was returned.

For once, since she was sitting at the front of the room, Reuben could gaze at Naomi to his heart's content, taking in every nuance of her expression as they sang the hymn that began every wedding he had ever been to.

Er hat ein Weib genommen,
　Die Christlich Kirch im Geist,
　Die Liebe hat ihn drungen,

Die er uns auch hat g'leist.
Sein Leben hat er vor uns g'stellt,
Die ihm auch also lieben
Sind ihm auch auserwahlt.

He has taken a wife
   The Christian Church in the Spirit,
   The love that so compelled him
   He also gave to us.
   Before us he's laid his life,
   So those who likewise love him
   Are also chosen for him.

Reuben watched the bride and groom come downstairs with the bishop and the preachers following the *abrot*, where they had been counseled about the solemnity and duties of marriage. His sister's head was humbly bowed as she took the bride's place on the bench next to her *neuwesitzern* and opposite her groom. The recitation of the weddings of the Old Testament held new meaning for Reuben now—especially poor Jacob working fourteen years for the woman he really loved. For the first time, he could see why Jacob had been willing to set aside his mistreatment at Laban's hands and buckle down and get to work.

When the service concluded and Julia and Zeph were husband and wife, Reuben was one of the helpers quickly turning the Miller living and dining rooms from a place of solemn ceremony to a place of joyful provision. The helpers set up the *eck* and the tables, the *eck leit* —the special friends and relatives who would serve the wedding party—decorated the tables as quickly as though they'd rehearsed it. Knowing Julia, they probably had. Then at last, he was able to take his place at the Miller family table, so close to where she sat in the *eck* that he could say her name and she would hear.

Naomi.

For a moment, he thought he'd really said it out loud, because she looked up, and her entire face seemed to glow with happiness and delight, just because he was there. Marlon, sitting next to him, followed his gaze and caught the tail end of his own smile, which he couldn't have suppressed even if Gabriel's trumpet had blown.

"So that's how it is, is it?" his eldest brother murmured. "Good for you."

"Nothing's settled," Reuben managed.

His brother chuckled. "I wouldn't say that. Naomi's a nice girl. Even *Mamm* likes her, and you know how she is."

Reuben did know. For strait was the gate and narrow was the way to *Mamm*'s good opinion, and few there were that found it. Only a partner with strength and a sincere heart was good enough for any of her *kinner*—or at least, that was what she'd told them when they neared the age of *Rumspringe*. "Choose as a date one who'd make a good mate," she'd told them, and though Reuben and his brothers had laughed and joked about it out in the barn where she couldn't hear, somehow the words had sunk in.

"I hear Naomi's going along on the wedding trip," Marlon said. "I thought I might go, too—at least as far as Colorado. There's a new church being established at Amity, and land prices are low enough I might be able to afford a few acres of my own, and some cattle to start a herd."

Their grandfather had built this house, and though space was getting tight as they grew up, it was still the only home Reuben had ever known. If he was going to ranch with his father and build a house for Naomi here, he mused, he'd build it up the slope a ways, on a knoll of ground that was protected by the hill behind it, yet looked out over the valley with a view all the way to the river. Then, once *Mamm* and *Dat* became too old to run cattle, this house could become the *daadi haus*.

"I don't think Naomi has made up her mind to go along yet." Reuben came back to the present to answer Marlon's remark. "Roy mentioned he might, though."

Marlon snorted. "Not if John Glick has anything to say about it."

And then the bishop bowed his head, the signal for a silent grace. They said no more during the meal because Marlon was clearly hungry and the elk roast was tasty enough to deserve a man's full attention. Following the massive meal, the bride and groom cut the cakes in the *eck,* and the servers went up and down the aisles between the tables laying out pies, cookies, and more cakes, all frosted in white or pale blue, to go with Julia's colors.

After lunch, Reuben and his brothers put up the benches and tables and got them into the bench wagon, which would eventually trundle off to Young Isaac Bontrager's for church the week after next, two days after Christmas.

After lunch, normally Reuben would amble out to the barn to visit with the men, or maybe have a game of darts with his friends in the tack room until it was time for the singing. But today, he didn't want to amble anywhere except to Naomi's side. He got as close as he could, but it wasn't easy, because as *neuwesitzern*, she and Lydia had their duties to perform.

With a small crowd of *maedscher*, they lured Julia out the mudroom door, only to squeal with delight as both her feet crossed the threshold. There, as she looked down, was a broom lying across the doorway.

"Welcome!" called Zeph's mother. "You're now one of us—a homemaker!"

Laughing, Julia picked up the brand-new broom, handmade by one of Zeph's brothers, and pretended to sweep *Mamm*'s newly sanded and varnished kitchen floor.

Julia and Zeph opened their gifts, with

Naomi keeping track of who had given what in the special book that had also been used for her shower. One of the gifts was a washing machine that had been converted to run on a gas engine, from all four of Zeph's uncles. Reuben had heard a rumor that Roy was the ringleader in a plot to get it up into the Miller loft via the hay hook. Maybe he'd succeed, maybe not. At least to Reuben's knowledge, he wasn't planning to put it on the roof of the barn, which would be quite a job since the barn had a steep peak. But he'd heard many a tale of bridal couples who'd had to get their machines down from crazy places like that before they could do their laundry on the Monday after the wedding.

But Reuben didn't really mind that Naomi was busy. He'd known she would be. The glow of that smile still lay on him like a beam of warm light, and he'd just visit and talk and bask in the memory of it all afternoon.

When it was time for the singing, his and David's small duty was to set out the *Ausbund* and their other hymnbooks. For once, Julia and Zeph didn't join in the singing—this time, they were sung to, and could just sit back, eat another piece of cake, and enjoy the sound of the *youngie*'s voices.

Reuben wasn't much of a singer, but every voice praised the *gut Gott* no matter how it sounded. And besides, when he sang a line like "I need Thee, oh, I need Thee, every hour I need Thee," it was completely impossible not to catch Naomi's eye and sing it as though to her. He would ask forgiveness of his Savior tonight. For now, the words expressed exactly how he felt.

When Julia and Zeph rose to hand out the cake favors, it was the signal for the *youngie* to take a break from singing. There would be more after supper. While Zeph carried the basket, Julia gave each of their guests a piece of wedding cake and thanked them for coming. With this, those who had the farthest to go or who had milking to do took their leave. He and his brothers still had to check that the cattle were all right in the barn, too, with twilight coming on, so Reuben took a moment to look in on Reggie.

He was bending next to him, untying the bandage to have a look at his healing leg, when the dog woofed softly in greeting.

Naomi was standing in the stall in her pristine white *kapp* and new blue dress with its matching cape and apron. Coatless, as he was. "How is he?"

"Careful out here. You don't want to get dirty. The day isn't over yet."

"I won't." She stepped closer to look over his shoulder.

Gently, he unwrapped the bandage. "He's healing up well. Who knew that Burn & Wound salve worked on coyote bites?"

"I guess we do, now."

The shoulder was looking good, too. "I can let him out of this stall tomorrow, but I'll keep him in the barn. Roaming around in here won't hurt him—and the horses will let him know if they don't like his trying to herd them." He fished his bandanna handkerchief out of his pocket and wiped his hands carefully. "You should go back. They'll be lining up for supper partners soon."

"I know. I just wanted to give you this first."

He turned around. "Wha—?" And before he could get out the rest of the word, she went up on tiptoe and kissed it into silence.

Her lips were soft as petals, and the world he was standing in just sort of faded away until all that existed was Naomi and this love in his heart that he'd never realized could be so powerful.

When she pulled away, it took him a second to remember where they were. Barn. Home. Wedding.

"When I go down to supper with Roy Beiler, and you go down with Grace, I want you to remember that," she whispered. Then she turned and slipped away as silently as she'd come.

———

THAT WAS WAY MORE *than a tiny bit forward, Naomi Glick.*

As she crossed the yard, Naomi had to laugh at how little good lecturing herself would do. When it came to Reuben Miller, she had just discovered she could be *very* forward, and now Reuben knew it. She wasn't one bit sorry. Kissing him had been glorious. What would it be like when he kissed her properly? She could hardly wait to find out.

Besides, she had only been taking the bride's good advice, hadn't she?

She was still hugging the memory of that kiss to herself when she joined the girls going into one bedroom upstairs, while the young men crowded into the other. Two by two, their names were called by Zeph's brother, who had been his *neuwesitzer*.

"Roy Beiler and Naomi Glick ... Reuben Miller and Grace Glick ... Darren Gingerich and Priscilla Yoder."

Hand in hand, as their names were called, they came down the stairs to take their places at dinner. Naomi caught Julia's eye and smiled so warmly that Julia looked a little surprised. She couldn't know about that *wunderbaar* moment in the barn, so she probably thought Naomi was reconciled to supper with Roy.

Naomi resisted the urge to laugh, then bowed her head in silent grace.

Roy was on his best behavior, it seemed, helping her to the bowls of mashed potatoes running with butter, the chicken pie, the

Christmas salad with its layers of red and green jelly sparkling with shredded carrot and cranberries.

"Nothing like a wedding for good food," he said, digging in.

"The district is small enough that everyone brings something," Naomi said by way of agreement. "The Christmas salad is so pretty. *Mamm* makes it every year."

Roy finished his plate before she was halfway through hers, then reached for seconds.

"Have you thought any more about going along on the honeymoon trip?" he asked.

"Not really." Other than the conviction that if he was going, she was not. "Have you?"

"I talked with your father about it the other night. He wasn't in favor."

"You must have known he wouldn't be," Naomi said. "If we have church in February, the house has to be completely finished inside, and that would be pretty hard to do with our carpenter gone for two weeks."

"That's what he said. And *I* said that I'd just work twice as hard while I was here, and I imagined the work would get done. Then *he* said I'd best keep my eyes on what I could see and not—"

"—what you imagined," Naomi finished for him. "*Dat* says that on occasion. Mostly to me."

"So, what I really need to know is whether you plan to go," he said, reaching for the beet pickles and spooning a couple on to his plate.

Naomi had been thinking of that trip as a way to get closer to Reuben, to share an adventure with him, and to make memories of something they might never do again. But now, everything was different. She could stay right here in Mountain Home, and every time she saw him would be an adventure—every memory something that would bring them closer.

Because he loved her. And that made every day a treasure she could count on.

"*Neh*," she said finally. "I don't think I'll go. Marlon Miller is going, and if you did, too, then it wouldn't be fitting, with two men and just me."

"How so?"

Did she have to spell it out for him? "It wouldn't be comfortable without another girl along. I don't think *Mamm* would let me go under those circumstances, anyway."

"But I'm your cousin," he objected. "And Marlon is way older than you and the bride's brother besides. Why would she have a problem with that?"

Because you want to be more than just my cousin, she thought. And there is no way I'm about to say that and give you any more ideas than you already have. "If you're going, I won't, and that's that."

He stared at her. "Ouch. I guess now I know what you really think of me."

"What I think of you doesn't matter," she said. "It's what *der Herr* thinks and what my parents think."

"Would you go if Reuben Miller was going?"

"Why should that make a difference?"

"You tell me."

She didn't owe him one thing, especially not an answer to that obnoxious question. "I'll tell you this—if you go off on a trip and leave *Dat* in the lurch, you for sure and certain won't have a job when you come back."

He laid his cutlery on his half empty plate

with a clank. "That's between me and John. You have a nice enough nose, but it doesn't belong in my business."

"It isn't," she said serenely. "I'm just telling you the truth."

As he pushed up from the table and headed to the bathroom, she looked up to see Reuben across the table and two places down, gazing at her over his glass of apple juice, which he was clearly drinking to disguise the grin on his face.

"Grace, can you cut me a piece of pie?" she asked her sister, who was sitting beside him.

"Cherry or sour grapes?" her sister inquired. Grace had ears like a cat, and the two of them had obviously heard the entire conversation.

"Oh, I think my supper partner already had a helping of that." She took the glistening piece of cherry goodness with a smile.

When Grace cut a second piece for Reuben, Naomi slid over into Roy's place so that she was nearly opposite the two of them. She forked up a satisfyingly big bite of pie. Reuben met her eyes as he, too, lifted his laden fork to his mouth. It was almost like sharing. And nothing had ever tasted so good.

Chapter 6

JULIA AND ZEPH had asked their parents if Old Christmas could be celebrated at the Miller place, with just the Yoder and Miller families, plus the Glicks. "It will bring our wedding party together again," Julia said to her mother, "and unite our families over a good meal for the first time since the wedding."

Of course, the parents on both sides had agreed, and now Reuben was wondering if maybe they shouldn't have sent the bench wagon away quite yet. Every chair they owned was occupied, as well as all the folding chairs, and still the *youngie* had elected to sit on the stairs or stand with their plates in their hands so that the older ones would have a place at the big table.

Their mothers and sisters had outdone themselves. Along with a big tom turkey that had been in the Yoders' freezer lockup since the autumn, *Mamm* had made the elk stew for which she was known all over the valley. Sharon Glick had brought a perfectly cured ham, and the assorted grandmothers saw to it that the table groaned with mashed potatoes, creamed corn, freshly baked bread, and pickles in all colors of the rainbow—green beans and cucumbers, carrots, beets, and even watermelon rind sent with best wishes from the Miller connections in Whinburg Township.

Reuben had seized his opportunity to find a place for himself and Naomi on the staircase. Their legs and feet were clearly visible to anyone who cared to look, but their heads were up high enough that he and Naomi could talk with at least the illusion of privacy.

That is, if the girls in their families would give them any.

Lydia and Amy Jane Glick were in the same

buddy bunch, which somehow meant they found the same things funny, and the two lovebirds billing and cooing on the stairs above were apparently hilarious.

"Just ignore them and maybe they'll go away," Reuben said in despair when his little *schweschder* had interrupted his attempts to speak for at least the fourth time.

"*Ach*, it's all right." Naomi slid a bean pickle off her fork onto his plate because she knew he liked them. "It's not every day there's a wedding in the family ... and besides, a little bird told me that Lydia might have a special friend here among us. I wonder who that could be?"

"It's not true!" Lydia protested, as though Naomi had actually been speaking to her. "I'm too young for all that, Naomi Glick. Reuben, don't you dare tell."

"Tell what?" He meant the question sincerely, since Naomi hadn't actually named names, but it had to be one of the Yoder boys. Lydia seemed to think he was demanding the young man's name.

"Come on, Amy Jane." Lydia got up. "Let's leave these two alone. I just saw *Mamm* go into the kitchen. I want another helping of stew in case she's counting."

They clattered down the stairs, leaving the gleaming wood risers blessedly empty.

"Peace, perfect peace, with loved ones far away," he murmured.

Naomi laughed. "You'd miss her if she was gone."

"That's true," he admitted. "But at least I can talk to you now without two other parties joining in."

"And what do you want to say?" Her eyes danced.

"It's not what, it's where." Somehow, in all this crowd, he would find a way to be alone with her and tell her some of what was in his heart.

She gave a mock sigh. "I suppose I can wait. Meanwhile, did you notice that Roy didn't come? *Mamm* made sure he knew, but she says he had another invitation."

"From who?"

"The Taylor boys, probably," she said, shaking her head. "Just a guess, but he has been spending some of his free time over there."

"I hope they stay out of our pastures, then. Does he still want to go along on the honeymoon trip?"

"I don't think so." Ever so lightly, she leaned her shoulder into his. "But if he does, that's his business. I'm finding life here very interesting lately, so I've no need to go."

"Glad to hear it." He paused. "Do you want to go for a walk?"

"Outside?"

"*Ja*, outside." He smiled into her eyes. "With all the people in here, you can't take a step without bumping into someone and risking them spilling their supper."

"All right. I'll just tell *Mamm*, and maybe she'll keep the younger ones from following us."

"They won't follow us," he said. "It's cold. But I want to show you something. Ask your opinion."

"Let me get my coat."

Naomi took his empty plate, and while she quietly stacked their plates in the kitchen, he found their coats and scarves. He jammed his feet into his boots and held the back door for her as they slipped outside.

"What do you want to show me?" She wrapped her scarf over her head and around her neck, and before she could locate her mittens in her coat pocket, he took her hand. "Oh, this is better than mittens," she said breathlessly.

Reggie, mostly recovered from his tussle with the coyotes, materialized out of the dark near the barn door, and loped along with them. Flashlight in hand, Reuben took the path that wound up the shallow slope from the river bottom where the house was. It had originally been a deer trail, but when his mother had planted her orchard not in the river valley, like most people thought she should, but in a sheltered and well-watered canyon up over the shoulder of this hill, the path had widened from years of frequent use.

Naomi kept pace with him easily, and he helped her over the slippery spots where snow had melted in the sun. The ground leveled into a wide meadow at the top of the knoll, and he led her over to the edge. "Here we are."

Beside him, her fingers still entwined in his, she gazed out at the lights of the house below and the bowl of twinkling stars overhead. Unseen in the darkness, the mountains surrounded their valley, offering protection and a kind of eternal watchfulness.

"I wish we had a moon."

"It's beautiful in full moonlight," he agreed. "If *Dat* and the *gut Gott* agree, maybe someday I'll build a house here."

"Really?" Her voice was soft. "It would be wonderful. Imagine looking out at this every day."

"I do," he said simply. "And I imagine *kinner* running all around, and maybe even a dog, and..."

"And?" she asked, sounding as though she could hardly speak the little word.

"And cows," he said thoughtfully. "Lots and lots of cows, grazing in the pastures and on the slopes of these mountains."

"Ah," she said wisely. "No life is complete without cows."

He turned serious at the hint of laughter in her voice. "I mean it, Naomi. I want to ranch here. It's a hard life, but it's one we both know. And I think with modern breeding and inoculation methods, I can increase our herds so that they will do more than just support the family. They'll provide money enough to build the house."

"You've talked this over with your father?"

"I have," he said. "A few days after the wedding, when he realized that Marlon doesn't intend to stay here and ranch with him. I don't think David does, either. He's got itchy feet. But I don't. I love this place. I want to stay here. With you."

"I want the same."

Her quiet words gave him the courage to speak again. "I wouldn't have gone on Julia and Zeph's honeymoon trip, anyway. Baptism classes start in February."

"I know. I'll be taking them."

"So, on Sunday I'm going to have a quiet word with Bishop Bontrager and ask if he'll include me, too."

She leaned against him, and still holding her hand, he tucked them both in his warm coat pocket.

"And after we're baptized," he went on, "I'll come courting. Because there was something missing in that picture I painted for you a minute ago."

"I noticed that," she said.

"No ranch is complete without a pretty, blue-eyed *fraa* to come home to."

"I'm sure it's the cows you mean."

He chuckled. "I could maybe live without cows if I had to. But I can't live without you."

"You won't ever have to," she whispered.

He squeezed her hand, safe and warm in his pocket. "For your parents' sake, I won't ask you the question that I want to ask right now, because we're not church members yet. But in the summer, let's make a promise that we'll come back up to this place, and I'll ask it then."

"I'll pack a picnic," she said. "I'll have the answer tucked away in my heart. And when I give it to you, it will be right here, where someday our home will be."

"Our home. I like the sound of that. Want to see something else?"

"I don't think you can improve on this view, Reuben Miller."

"It's not a view." He released her hand and tugged the flashlight and a piece of paper out of his other pocket. "When I was talking with *Dat,* we decided that if I went in as a partner with him, we ought to have a name for the ranch, and a proper brand." Shining the beam on the paper, he asked, "What do you think?"

She gazed at it. "The Circle M?"

He knew she'd recognize the double message as soon as she laid eyes on it—the M shaped like the double peak of the mountain behind them. "*Ja.* Our new brand. I'll register it with the county as soon as the offices open next week."

"I like it. The *M* for Miller, and the circle for love."

"Exactly. All around us, protecting us. Love, family, and most of all, *der Herr* who loves us and gives us a Christmas miracle when we least expect it."

She went into his arms, nestling there as though she had found the place where she belonged. Then she stiffened with a gasp.

"What is it?" he said in sudden alarm.

"I never made you a gift!"

He tipped back his head and laughed. Then he wrapped his arms around her and spoke into the scarf over her ear. "But God made sure that you did. The only Christmas gift I wanted was to hold you like this and know that you'll be mine forever."

This Christmas, and every Christmas to come for as long as the *gut Gott* gave them.

And there in the high country they both loved, in the place where he would build her a home, he kissed her the way a man kisses the woman he intends to make his wife. With joy, and humility, and a promise as eternal as the stars twinkling in the wide Montana sky.

THE END

Afterword

Dear reader,

I hope you've enjoyed this prequel novella about how the Miller family began on the Circle M Ranch. If you subscribe to my newsletter www.subscribepage.com/shelley-adina, you'll hear about new releases in the series, my research in Montana, and snippets about quilting and writing and chickens—my favorite subjects!

And I invite you to visit my online store at www.moonshellbooks.com. While you're there, be sure to browse my other Amish novels set in beautiful Whinburg Township, Pennsylvania, beginning with *The Wounded Heart.*

And now, I hope you'll turn the page for an excerpt from *The Amish Cowboy*, book one in the Amish Cowboys series featuring Reuben and Naomi's eldest son Daniel ... and the girl who got away ...

Excerpt
THE AMISH COWBOY © ADINA SENFT

Mountain Home, Montana

"God is good, and northwestern Montana is the proof."

Daniel Miller laid a hand on his mare's neck as she sidestepped, and gazed out at the forests and meadows of the high country, with Siksika Lake set like a jewel in the cupped hands of the mountains. They had brought the horses to a halt on a knoll that Daniel knew was one of Dat's favorite places to give thanks, as he was doing now. Above them, a hawk balanced on the updraft created by the looming bulk of the mountain, and off to the left, deer grazed on one side of a grassy clearing.

Behind them in the acres of the collection field, cattle milled and lowed, the females looking to mother up with their calves, calves bawling as they tried to find the mothers they'd been separated from when the cowboys had brought them down from the forests and meadows of the high country over the past week.

Daniel's father, Reuben, pushed up the brim of his black winter work hat with one gloved finger. "We have a lot to be thankful for. That the *gut Gott* made this country. That He led me here when my brothers were determined that I follow them to Colorado and New Mexico. And that He gave me and your *mamm* a fine family to help us care for it."

"I'll agree with you on all but the last one. I think the *gut Gott* might have been distracted when it came to making the twins."

Reuben laughed. "I must say that those girls are a handful—worse than you four boys together. But they seemed to have settled some now. Rebecca plans to start baptism classes and join church in the spring, she tells me."

"Does she?" Daniel's heart swelled, and the sun seemed to lie with greater warmth on his shoulders. "Let's hope Malena takes her good example to heart."

"She is in God's hands, *mei Sohn*, and there is no safer place."

Reuben gathered up his gelding's reins and they rode down the path single file, the horses sensing instinctively that today's inspection of the cattle was over, and it was time to go home. In Amish communities in other states, the elders frowned on riding horses, which were meant to pull buggies and to work in the fields. But Amish communities in other states didn't sprawl across mountains with steep sides and narrow trails. If a rancher did not hold with gas-powered quad-runners—noisy, smelly things that only frightened the cattle—then using a horse for riding was certainly the lesser of two evils. So, the Circle M kept cutting horses for ranch work, and buggy horses for transportation.

Daniel patted Marigold's neck again in

appreciation. The twins had named the cutting horses after flowers, regardless of what their actual names had been at the time, and Dat had laughed and gone along with it. Daniel supposed he should be thankful they'd stopped before they got to Skunk Cabbage or Hydrangea.

He gazed up at the ranks of the Rockies marching into the distance, their jagged peaks white with new snow. "So, Dat, we start trailing them down day after tomorrow? Rafe Williams at the Bar Z has already taken his, and I expect John Mackenzie will follow soon."

His father nodded. The trails were already trampled from the movement of their neighbors' herds. "*Ja*, it's time. The Bar Z and the Star are bigger outfits than we are, so it's right they started early. Our neighbors and some in the church are just waiting for us to give the word. The weather isn't supposed to change until next week, but it's October. You know how that goes."

Montana weather was notoriously unpredictable, and even though the last week of September had been warm, since then there had been a skiff of snow down in the home paddocks. Daniel was grateful for their neighbors, both *Englisch* and Amish, who considered roundup a community event. All the neighboring ranches ran their cattle on the surrounding allotments. They weren't fenced, so the animals could get to the grazing land, and the animals often wandered on to the Bureau of Land Management land as well. Sorting one ranch's cattle from another took place in the collection fields, where it was manageable, and now his family were ready for the final stage of the process: trailing their own cattle down to the Circle M seven miles away.

The steep trail widened out as they reached the open country. Daniel inspected the way, looking for washouts or mud holes that might snag an unsuspecting calf or cause a neighbor's horse to throw an inexperienced rider or injure itself. But with the herds coming down so recently, the wide track was plain and unobstructed. At the gate that gave on to the county road, Daniel allowed his father to ride through first, then closed and secured the gate behind them both.

The law of the gate, he had learned even before he was old enough to reach the latch, meant that you left it as you found it. Always. No exceptions.

After four miles along the road, the horses broke into a trot when they saw the familiar fences and fields of home in the distance. His own half-constructed house lay just visible to the west, its roof and walls newly dried in and waiting for the many hours of elbow grease he'd put in during the short days and long evenings of winter. The sight always gave Daniel a pang of happiness at homecoming, with a soft edge of longing. Longing for a wife, a partner who would share the joys and burdens of life with him, doubling the one and halving the other. For children they might bring up in the fear of the Lord, teaching them the Amish ways that had been handed down for hundreds of years.

Unbidden, her face flashed into his memory —those gray eyes, the pain in them as she told him she could not marry him. Lovina Wengerd Lapp had stayed in Whinburg Township where it was safe, and married someone else. Not a cowboy whose life on the ranch could sometimes be as difficult as it was rewarding, but a baker or a harness maker or something. A man who stayed inside to make his living.

Daniel shook away the unkind memories and allowed the beauty of the country to soak into his soul. His parents' ranch house stood on a slight rise farther up the valley, facing south, to gather in as much light and warmth as possible during short winter days. Daadi Miller, and the teenage Reuben with his two brothers Marlon and David, had built it in the seventies when their family had settled here, an easy buggy ride to the town of Mountain Home. More and more families had come to settle, and now the *Englisch* tourists were coming to enjoy the homemade goods at the bakery, the variety in the general store, the handcrafted ironwork and quilts. Their own log house with its peaked roof jutting out over the front deck seemed to welcome visitors, and on church Sundays the front room held all the *Gmay*, with the view through the windows of the land God had created, to remind them of all they had to be grateful for.

The bunkhouse and cattle barns, and his

own house as well, were constructed using the same methods, out of sturdy logs with corrugated metal roofs that would let snow slide harmlessly away. Even the chicken house fit the pattern, large enough for the fifty birds and the few speckled guinea hens that were cared for by Mamm and the twins.

After unsaddling the horses, currying them, and putting them in their stalls with the feed they'd been hoping for, Reuben told him, "I'll make those calls. No sense wasting time."

Other Amish communities might have a telephone hanging in the barn, or in a phone shanty out on the road. But here in Montana, life was a little more challenging than in the older, more established communities in Indiana and Pennsylvania and Ohio. Between high country and weather, and the distance between families, it had become clear to the elders both here and in Colorado that cell phones were necessary for safety. There was even a cell tower on the Stolzfus place that brought a little extra income from the phone company to the widow Rose.

So while Dat leaned on a post in the barn to

make his calls, watching the horses enjoy their oats, Daniel walked up to the house.

"You're back!" Malena met him at the door and then hollered over her shoulder, "Mamm, Daniel and Dat are back."

"Don't sound so surprised." He grinned at his sister, who was twenty-two, but whose merry eyes and small figure made her look still in her teens. Her prayer covering was neatly pinned on curly brown hair that never stayed quite as neat as Rebecca's straighter hair seemed to, a fact that caused significant aggravation every church Sunday.

"I'm not surprised. I'm glad." Malena hugged him, a brief, fierce hug that nearly squeezed the breath out of him. "When is roundup?"

"Day after tomorrow."

She whooped and grabbed a barn coat off the hook. "I'll tell the boys."

"Dat is out there, he will—"

But she was already out the door, and here came Rebecca down the stairs from their room. "Tomorrow? Goodness, I've got to get Lilac ready then, and clean her tack, and—"

Another barn jacket vanished and the door slammed behind her.

"And they say there are no tornadoes in Montana," he said into the silence. Daniel heard a quiet chuckle and turned to see his mother in the kitchen doorway, wiping her hands on a dish towel.

Naomi Miller smiled a welcome, and tilted her head toward the kitchen. "Gingerbread whoopie pies cooling on the counter. One thing about your sisters—any job they tackle gets done in a hurry."

"Even if you have to make them do it over again?" He took a whoopie pie and the warm scent of ginger and cream-cheese frosting filled his nose as he bit into it.

"Not so much anymore. Even Malena learned eventually that if you do something properly the first time, you have more time afterward to do your own things. Simple arithmetic. And at least they got the pies done. I only have to frost the rest and put them together."

"These are good." Daniel took another. "Dat's in the barn making the calls. Day after tomorrow."

Mamm nodded. "We'll give everyone breakfast, as usual. We've got elk sausage, bacon and mushroom casserole, and a couple of pigs' weight in pork sausage. That should hold you all until lunch."

"You and the girls are riding out, too?"

"The girls wouldn't miss this. But I'll stay here with the women who aren't riding." She brushed a bit of frosting from the stubble on his cheek. "You need a shave if you're going to catch a girl's eye, *mei Sohn*."

"Hey, I've been chasing cattle for two days," he defended himself. As if she couldn't tell by the smell of horse and the stains on his jeans. "Besides, all the girls in this neck of the woods have their eyes on someone else. I've got used to being the third oldest bachelor in the district."

"Third? Who might the first two be?" She was trying not to smile, and failing completely.

"Josiah and John Bontrager."

His mother's laughter always delighted Daniel. It sounded like a rushing creek and birdsong and kindness, if that were possible. "Those old bachelors! They've got forty years on you and even yet, I know a widow or two who would light a candle in the window if she thought one would come calling."

Now it was his turn to laugh. "I'm barely twenty-eight, Mamm. When God sends me the woman He means for me, I'll be ready and waiting."

His mother had crossed the kitchen and bent to open the propane oven's door, which was why he thought she said, "He already did."

But that couldn't be right. Mamm had never met Lovina Lapp.

Chapter 2

Two days later, the entire Miller family was up and at work by four a.m. While the twins helped Mamm in the kitchen, preparing an enormous breakfast for twenty people, Daniel and his brothers went down to the barn to get the horses tacked up and ready. Well, Zach and Adam were helping. Joshua, who at twenty-one was the youngest of his brothers, had a gift for finding something to do that wasn't the task at hand, and managed to skate out from under the work his brothers did.

Not today. Daniel set him to preparing trail bundles.

"What for?" Joshua wanted to know. "It's not like we're going to be camping up there like last week. We'll be back by nightfall."

"Never hurts to be prepared." Daniel handed him a stack of waterproof stuff bags. "There could be a freak blizzard, like the one four years ago. What would have happened to you then if we hadn't had tents and camping mats?"

"I'd be dead, probably. Frozen solid until spring." That was one thing about Josh. Daniel could usually get him to see reason. Once he saw it, he was more happy to do what was asked of him. But if he couldn't see the reason for something, he was as slippery as a calf in a mudhole and usually went scrambling off in another direction.

"Besides, the horses carry the extra," Adam pointed out, invisible behind a stall wall, where he was checking his horse's feet. "Not like anyone is asking you to pack it all in on your back."

"Everyone carries their own lunches. No chuck wagon this year?" Zach pushed his glasses up with a gesture similar to the one Dat used to adjust his hat. At twenty-six, Zach was the next in age to Daniel. It was comical how much he was like their father in body, and how far apart they were in other ways. While Dat loved the land and the animals it nurtured, Zach was interested in the homes people lived in. He'd been nagging the folks over at Meadowlark to take him on as a member of their crew so he could learn the ins and outs of building log houses, but hadn't succeeded yet. Now, at the end of the building season, he'd have to wait until spring. Maybe that was God's will, too, along with finding a partner in life.

"Neh, we're leaving the chuck wagon home." Daniel lifted down the camping mats and the pup tents. Two people fit comfortably in a tent. He'd spent more than one night in the meadows of the high country in the spring, talking over life with Adam, his middle brother, or Zach, in the shelter of one of these tents. They weren't meant for long-term camping. They were just in case of the unexpected. "Best

go find the backpacks. I think they're in the office closet."

Zach returned a few minutes later. "I'll run these up to Mamm so the girls can fill them after breakfast."

Some ranchers' allotments were farther away than a day's ride, so they'd use a chuck wagon. Not like the old relics Daniel had seen in history books. Rather, it was an enclosed vehicle that had been an Amish buggy in a former life, now fitted out with a camp stove, propane tank, and storage for food and pans. It lived at Bishop Wengerd's place and was rolled out whenever it was needed.

There was that pang in his heart again. Daniel shook his head at himself as he heaved a saddle on to Marigold's blanketed back. Wengerd had been Lovina's maiden name. The two families were related, but "Little Joe" Wengerd, the six-foot-five head of the Montana branch of the family and their community's bishop, hadn't been back to Whinburg Township in thirty years. Some thought it was because he'd had a falling-out with his brother, Lovina's grandfather. Others that he disliked travel by train. But Little Joe had once told Daniel that it was because of the cattle.

"Hard to leave 'em," he'd said. "Can't just go away for a month in any season. The Lord has made me responsible for 'em, as well as for the church, so I've got to be a good husbandman to both and stay where He's put me."

Bless Little Joe, who pressed into the center of God's will. It was pointless to think about Lovina. Worse than pointless—it was a little too close to complaining about that same will. God's will was perfect, and Lovina was living within it. What Daniel needed to do was draw closer, too, like Little Joe. Only there would he find the peace he craved.

———

By six a.m. the sky glowed, telling them sunrise wasn't far away and making the quaking aspens turn molten gold with reflected light. Mist rose from the home fields, where the fences looked like ghosts, the white vapor eddying with the movement of the buggy horses, who would not be going along. Joshua and a couple of the younger teenage boys ran hither and yon, doing last-minute tasks that no one had asked for, while *Englisch* and Amish neighbors came riding or driving up the gravel lane in twos and threes.

Daniel felt as though he ought to be mounted up, riding the edge of the milling crowd to keep them all together, the way he did the cattle before Dat whistled and headed out. Instead, he was trying not to look at his sisters' getups—they wore jeans and boots under their modest dresses so that they could ride astride. Both girls had tied scarves over their braided buns, with shapeless hats on top to keep off the sun later, and keep their heads warm now. The air was frigid, frost riming the roofs of the buildings and edging every vein in the fallen leaves. They all had their winter coats on, and Daniel was thankful his horse would help keep his legs warm until the sun was properly up.

Here came the Wengerd party, the bishop with his snow-white beard leading the way. He'd already brought his animals down to his own ranch with the Millers' help. It would never occur to him not to return the favor.

Among the buggies was one driven by his wife, Sadie, accompanied by her youngest daughter Ruby and what looked like another woman. Another buggy was driven by one of her daughters-in-law and brought Sadie's grandchildren, while her two grown sons rode. And what was this? Who belonged to the little boy riding an old horse so stiffly in front of Little Joe's eldest son? Neither of the sons had a boy big enough to—

The buggies rolled to a stop and the occupants spilled out.

"Mamm! Mamm, did you see? Cousin Peter let me ride the whole way all by myself!"

A laughing woman looked up at the excited boy and laid a hand on his leg. "You did so well, and the horse obeyed you."

"He's a natural," Peter Wengerd said, leaning on his saddle horn while Daniel's heart came to a complete halt in his chest.

As though a gong had rung to get her attention, the boy's mother turned, and for the second time in his life, Daniel Miller was poleaxed by a pair of gray eyes, starred with long lashes that had once given him "butterfly kisses" all over his face. Those graceful hands had once cupped his jaw. That rose-petal mouth had once said things to make a man's heart burn with hope ... and in the end said words that had simply burned.

Lovina-love.

Her face had gone white as frost, and yet she did not look away.

"Daniel!" Adam and Zach flanked him. "Daniel? Hey!" Adam squeezed his arm. *"Was ischt?"*

All at once the sounds of horses stamping, neighbors talking, and harness jingling flooded into his ears. His feet in their sturdy Western boots were firmly on the ground, and he was no longer floating in some cloudlike place where only the two of them existed.

"What?" he said.

"Little Joe says some of their company might want to come along. They only got here yesterday."

They'd arrived yesterday? Had she been here a whole day and he had not known?

Don't be an idiot, he told himself. There's no connection between you anymore. She is married and clearly that is her child and there's an end of it. Her husband was probably one of the riders still coming in, or maybe he was driving a buggy.

And now here they came, to greet Dat and Mamm. When she had spoken to them and given them the Whinburg connections' greetings, she turned to him.

"Daniel," she said.

His heart did a kind of belly-flop in his chest at the sound of his name in that musical voice. "Lovina. Welcome to the Circle M. Is that your boy?"

For answer, she turned. "Joel! *Kumm hier.*"

The boy ran up obediently. Here were Lovina's gray eyes under a mop of chocolate-brown hair. That must come from her husband, because her hair was as fair and shining as a skein of silk.

"Joel, this is Daniel Miller, Reuben's oldest son."

The boy ducked his head. *"Guder mariye,* Daniel. *Denki* for letting us come today."

He wasn't aware he had. "I'm glad you could. But how—" *How did you come to be here at all?*

"It's a long story," she said, "but the short version is that we joined a party of people who hired an *Englisch* van for a touring holiday."

"We've seen eight national parks out of twelve," Joel said eagerly. "At Yellowstone we saw the geyser. And at Glacier there was a big bear and a herd of elk and—" He stopped. "And then the van died."

"So I borrowed someone's phone to call Cousin Joe and he told us the Amtrak stops at Libby. We have to make arrangements to travel home." A flush burned into her face. "I had no idea that we would be interrupting the ranch work in this way."

"You aren't interrupting," Little Joe rumbled, coming up behind her in time to hear. "It'll be good for you to get up into God's country."

"But we're not going," she protested. "I said I would help with the cooking."

Little Joe looked down at her, compassion written in his face. "You need a change, cousin. To take your mind off … everything."

"He means my *dat*," Joel supplied somberly, looking up at Daniel. "The national parks were supposed to do that, but even when I saw the geyser, all I could think was how he would have liked it."

Lovina bent to hug him. "Of course you think of him, and you should. He was a good man who deserves our good memories. But *der Herr* decided that it was Dat's time, and so we must accept His will."

He *would have* liked it? *Dat's time?* Did that mean—

Daniel's heart did a swan dive off a high precipice.

Lovina Lapp was a widow?

———

Look for The Amish Cowboy at your favorite online retailer, or on my store at moonshellbooks.com!

Glossary

Spelling and definitions from Eugene S. Stine, *Pennsylvania German Dictionary* (Birdboro, PA: Pennsylvania German Society, 1996).

Words used:
der Herr the Lord
dochsder daughter
druwwel trouble
duchly headscarf
Englisch non-Amish people, the English language
faulenzer lazy person
fress midnight snack

Gmay congregation

Gott God

guder owed, wie geht's? good afternoon, how's it going?

gut good

hochmut proud

ja yes

kinner children

lieber Vater dear Father

maedscher young girls

mei bruder my brother

neh no

neuwesitzer lit. side-sitter, or bridal supporter

Rumspringe The time of running around for Amish youth

schweschder(e) sister, sisters

wunderbaar wonderful

Also by Adina Senft

Amish Cowboys of Montana

The Amish Cowboy's Christmas prequel novella

The Amish Cowboy

The Amish Cowboy's Baby

The Amish Cowboy's Bride

The Amish Cowboy's Letter

The Amish Cowboy's Makeover

The Amish Cowboy's Home

The Amish Cowboy's Refuge

The Amish Cowboy's Mistake

The Amish Cowboy's Little Matchmakers

The Amish Cowboy's Wedding Quilt

The Amish Cowboy's Journey

———

The Whinburg Township Amish

The Wounded Heart

The Hidden Life

The Tempted Soul

Herb of Grace

Keys of Heaven

Balm of Gilead

The Longest Road

The Highest Mountain

The Sweetest Song

The Heart's Return (novella)

———

Breaking Faith

Grounds to Believe

Pocketful of Pearls

Sounds in the Night

Over Her Head

———

Glory Prep (faith-based young adult)

Glory Prep

The Fruit of My Lipstick

Be Strong and Curvaceous

Who Made You a Princess?

Tidings of Great Boys

The Chic Shall Inherit the Earth

About the Author

USA Today bestselling author Adina Senft grew up in a plain house church, where she was often asked by outsiders if she was Amish (the answer was no). She holds a PhD in Creative Writing from Lancaster University in the UK. Adina was the winner of RWA's RITA Award for Best Inspirational Novel in 2005 for *Grounds to Believe*, a finalist for that award in 2006 for *Pocketful of Pearls*, and was a Christy Award finalist in 2009 for *The Fruit of My Lipstick*. She appeared in the 2016 documentary film *Love Between the Covers*, is a popular speaker and convention panelist, and has been a guest on many podcasts, including Worldshapers and Realm of Books.

She writes steampunk adventure and mystery as Shelley Adina; and as Charlotte Henry, writes classic Regency romance. When she's not writing, Adina is usually quilting, sewing historical costumes, or enjoying the garden with her flock of rescued chickens.

Adina loves to talk with readers about books, quilting, and chickens!
www.moonshellbooks.com

facebook.com/adinasenft

pinterest.com/shelleyadina

bookbub.com/authors/adina-senft

instagram.com/shelleyadinasenft

bsky.app/profile/shelleyadinasenft.bsky.social

Made in the USA
Middletown, DE
05 March 2025

72312067R00083